THE KING'S TEA

Weekly Reader Children's Book Club presents

TRINKA HAKES NOBLE
THE KING'S TEA

THE DIAL PRESS / NEW YORK

Published by
The Dial Press
1 Dag Hammarskjold Plaza
New York, New York 10017

Copyright © 1979 by Trinka Hakes Noble
All rights reserved. Manufactured in the U.S.A.
Design by Atha Tehon

Library of Congress Cataloging in Publication Data
Noble, Trinka Hakes. The king's tea.
Summary: The King's day is ruined when the milk for
his tea is sour and nobody wants to take the blame.
[1. Kings, queens, rulers, etc.—Fiction] I. Title
PZ7. N6715Ki [E] 79-50749
ISBN 0-8037-4529-X ISBN 0-8037-4530-3 lib. bdg.

For Randon, with love

The King's tea had to be perfect.

But sometimes things weren't just right. So each morning the tea steward held his breath as the King took his first sip. . . .

"Blaaa!" shouted the King. "This tea's not perfect. The milk is sour. Now my day is ruined, and it's all your fault!"

With that the King slammed down his cup and stomped out for a morning walk.

The tea steward picked up the pitcher of milk and hurried off to see the cook. "Cook, I told you to get me sweet milk," scolded the steward. "Now the King's tea is ruined, and it's all your fault!"

The cook turned in a huff and shook a wooden spoon at the kitchen girl.

"Girl, I've told you again and again to bring me sweet milk! Now the King's tea is ruined, and it's all your fault!"

The poor girl quickly slipped out the door into the yard.

There she met the farmer who delivered the milk to the castle each day.

"Farmer, you have delivered sour milk and ruined the King's tea. Now the cook is angry with me, and it's all your fault!"

When the farmer got home, he went to the creamery to see his wife.
"Wife," he said crossly. "You gave me sour milk this morning, and I delivered it to the castle. Now the King's tea is ruined, and it's all your fault!"

The farmer's wife turned to the boy and seized him by the ear.

"Boy, listen to me well," she said. "You brought me sour milk which I gave to my husband, who took it to the castle. Now the King's tea is ruined, and it's all your fault!"

The boy ran to the meadow to see the cow.

"You nasty old cow," shouted the boy. "You gave me sour milk this morning which I gave to the farmer's wife, who gave it to her husband, who took it to the castle. Now the King's tea is ruined, and you are to blame!"

"Don't blame me," mooed the cow. "Blame the yellow buttercups. They are not very sweet this spring, so it's all their fault!"

The King had also gone to the meadow that morning and he overheard every-
thing the boy and the cow said.

"The King's tea? Sour milk? Oh, my . . ." said the King. So when the boy and
the cow went to see the buttercups, the King decided to follow.

"Buttercups," bellowed the cow. "My milk is sour and it's all your fault!"
The buttercups looked shriveled and dry.
"It's not their fault," said the boy. "They need the gentle spring rain to make them sweet."

A dark cloud in the sky overheard the boy.

"Everyone is always blaming the weather," rumbled the cloud. "If rain is what they want, then rain they shall have."

The dark cloud moved over the buttercups, and soft raindrops fell. The buttercups soaked up the sweet rain, and the cow began to eat.

"It's not always the weather's fault," thundered the cloud as it rolled on over the meadow.

The cow ate and ate until she had eaten her way across the meadow to the spot where the King was picking buttercups. She was still hungry.

"I hope you don't mind if I eat that bouquet of buttercups you're holding," said the cow, who had never before seen the King. "If I don't eat enough buttercups, my milk will not be sweet, and that would ruin the King's afternoon tea."

"Did you say afternoon tea? What a pleasant thought," said the King. "Of course you may eat my bouquet. The King's tea must be perfect!"

So he let the cow eat his bouquet and strolled off toward his castle.

Later that day the boy milked the cow and carried the milk to the creamery. There the farmer's wife strained the milk and gave it to her husband, who delivered it to the castle.

The kitchen girl carried the milk to the cook, who poured it into a pitcher and gave it to the tea steward, who hurried off to set it on the table just in time for the King's afternoon tea.

But the King didn't take his first sip right away. Instead he invited the tea steward to tea.

The tea steward invited the cook, who invited the girl,

who invited the farmer, who invited his wife,

who invited the boy, who ran to the meadow and invited the cow,

who brought buttercups for everyone! And as they took their first sip, they agreed
that the King's tea was delicious.

"No, no. Not delicious," said the King, laughing. "It's perfect!"

TRINKA HAKES NOBLE

grew up in rural southern Michigan. She has always been interested in art and began to study drawing when she was in junior high school. Ms. Noble attended Michigan State University and, after graduation, taught art in Michigan, Virginia, and Rhode Island. For the past three years she has studied illustration at Caldecott medalist Uri Shulevitz's workshop.

Ms. Noble now lives with her husband and daughter in Upper Montclair, New Jersey.